Junie B., First Grader®
BOO...and I MEAN It!

BARBARA PARK

Junie B., First Grader® BOO...and I MEAN It!

illustrated by Denise Brunkus

SCHOLASTIC INC.

New York Toronto London Auckland Sydney
Mexico City New Delhi Hong Kong Buenos Aires

To "Jodi B." Reamer, who, I am convinced,
is Junie B.'s big sister in a parallel universe.
Thanks for your friendship, your advice,
and—most of all—your laughter.

ISBN 0-439-79390-4

Text copyright © 2004 by Barbara Park. Illustrations copyright © 2004 by Denise Brunkus. All rights reserved. Published by Scholastic Inc., 557 Broadway, New York, NY 10012, by arrangement with Random House Children's Books, a division of Random House, Inc. SCHOLASTIC and associated logos are trademarks and/or registered trademarks of Scholastic Inc.

12 11 10 9 8 7 6 5 4 3 2 1   5 6 7 8 9 10/0

Printed in the U.S.A.   40

First Scholastic printing, October 2005

Contents

1

Secrets

Friday

Dear first-grade journal,

My daddy went away on
~~business~~
a ~~biznus~~ trip this week. He is
doing job ~~intervus~~. interviews

Job ~~intervus~~ is when you put interviews
on a suit. And you wear a tie.
And you beg people for a job.

I wish Daddy did not have to
do job ~~intervus~~ right now. interviews

1

'Cause HALLOWEEN is coming tomorrow!

And I am afraid of that scary holiday!

From,

Scaredy Junie B.,

First Grader

P.S. I am not telling anyone that I am scared of halloween. Or else, they will ~~teeze~~ tease me . . . probably.

Children are like that.

I put down my pencil and thought about Halloween some more.

Then I did a little shiver.

On account of last year, a boy named Paulie Allen Puffer told me five scary secrets about that day. And he said I am not allowed to tell anyone. Or else a witch will turn my head into a wart.

I made a sick face. And I tried not to think about that situation.

Only how can you not think about a situation if you're trying not to think about a situation?

I tapped my fingers very frustrated.

Then, all of a sudden, I saw my journal on my desk. And a good idea came in my head. 'Cause sometimes if you write your problems in a journal, it makes you feel better about things.

I heard that on the Home Shopping Network. They were selling journals, I believe.

I quick opened the pages. And I started to write.

    5 scary secrets that
    Paulie Allen Puffer told me
    by Junie B. Jones

(1.) Real monsters and witches go trick or treating on halloween. Only they don't even wear costumes. ~~costooms~~. On account of everybody thinks they're already dressed up.
    BUT THEY'RE NOT! THEY ARE WEARING THEIR REAL ACTUAL FACE AND CLOTHES!

4

②Do not carve pointy, sharp teeth in your pumpkin. Or else it will roll into your room while you are sleeping and eat your feet.

③ Bats like to land on your head and live in your hair.

④ Black witch cats can claw you into shreddle.

⑤ Candy corn isn't really corn.

I put down my pencil again. And I read over the secrets.

That candy corn one is shocking, I tell you.

Writing my problems did not make me feel better.

I put my head on my desk. And I covered up with my arms.

Just then, I heard my teacher's voice.

His name is Mr. Scary.

That is a good Halloween name, I think. Only he actually uses it for the whole entire year.

He said to please take out our arithmetic books.

I kept on staying covered up.

'Cause how can I do arithmetic when there's scary secrets in my brain?

All around me, Room One got out their books.

I took my sweatshirt from the back of my chair. And I tucked it next to my ears.

Sweatshirts help block out classroom noise.

Pretty soon, I heard my teacher again.

"Junie B.? Are you all right back there?" he asked.

Only before I could even answer, a tattletale girl named May started blabbing her head off!

"*No*, Mr. Scary! Junie Jones is *not* all right," she said. "Junie Jones is not paying attention again . . . as *usual*."

She thought for a second.

"And Junie Jones has been doing *other* bad stuff lately, too," she said. "Like yesterday she ate half a sandwich from her lunch box during silent reading. Only I couldn't even tattle on her. Because you said if I keep on tattling, I'll get a note sent home. And so thank goodness that you were finally on the ball today."

After that, Room One got very silent. And Mr. Scary didn't say any words.

I felt shaky inside.

He was thinking of a punishment for me, probably.

Finally, I raised my head. And I peeked one eye at him.

He was sitting at his desk writing a note.

I did a groan.

It was to my mother, I think.

I started to hide my eye again.

Only just then, Mr. Scary stood up very calm.

And he came to the back of the room.

And gave the note to *May*!

I could not believe my eyeball!

"Please take this home to your parents," he told her.

May's whole mouth came open at that shocking news.

"No, Mr. Scary! No, no, no! Please don't make me take a note! Please! Please! Please! I wasn't *tattling*! I *promise* I wasn't! I was just saying that I'm glad

you're on the ball today! That's all I was saying. I was saying that I am *glad* for you."

Mr. Scary smiled. "Thank you, May. You're very kind," he said.

Then he bent down next to her. And he stuck the note in her backpack.

I reached over and tapped on him.

"That note was long overdue," I said.

Mr. Scary sucked in his cheeks at me.

"Please sit up, Junie B.," he said.

His voice did not sound happy.

"*Now,*" he said.

I quick sat up.

"Okey-doke. I'm sitting. See me sitting, Mr. Scary?" I said. "Plus also, I am going to get out my arithmetic book, I think."

I found it in my backpack.

"Yessiree! Here it is. I've got my book.

And so I am all set to do arithmetic now," I said.

Mr. Scary kept on standing there.

I looked up at him.

"All rightie. You can be heading on back to your desk," I said.

He still did not move.

I waved my fingers.

"Keep in touch," I said.

Mr. Scary bent down next to me. And he talked real serious in my ear.

"You need to pay attention in class, Junie B.," he said. "I shouldn't have to tell you that."

I did a sigh.

Then I leaned over. And I whispered to him real private.

"Yeah, only I've got something in my head that's bothering me today," I explained. "On account of scary Halloween is coming tomorrow. And I don't actually like it that much."

Just then, May's ears perked up.

That girl has X-ray hearing, I tell you.

"Hey, everybody! Junie Jones is *scared* of Halloween!" she shouted. "I just heard her say it! Junie Jones is a scaredy-cat baby about Halloween!"

All of Room One turned around and looked at me.

"Really?" said my bestest friend named Herbert. "You're scared of Halloween, Junie B.? I didn't know that."

"I didn't know that, either," said my other friend named Shirley. "How come you're scared of Halloween?"

Just then, a boy named Sheldon jumped up at his desk. And he talked real loud.

"Well, *I'm* not scared of Halloween. *That's* for sure!" he said.

He stood there a second.

Then he did a little frown.

"Except for last year, Daniel Delmonte dressed up like Mr. Potato Head. And he jumped out at me from a bush. And so I had to drop my bag and run."

Room One laughed and laughed.

Sheldon frowned bigger.

"It wasn't funny," he said. "I had to start my candy from scratch."

May rolled her eyes.

"Who cares, Sheldon?" she said. "The thing is that Junie Jones is scared of Halloween *this* year! And that makes her a scaredy-cat baby."

She leaned across the aisle at me.

"B-A-B-Y spells *baby,*" she said.

I crossed my arms at that girl.

"Oh, yeah? Well, T-A-T-L-T-A-I-L spells *tattletale*," I said back.

Mr. Scary looked down at me.

He shook his head no.

I thought for a second.

Then I tried again.

"T-A-T-A-L-T-A-L-E spells *tattletale*," I said.

Mr. Scary did a wince.

I tapped my fingers on my desk.

Then I took one more crack at it.

"T-A-T-A-L-T-A-I-L spells *tattletale*?"

Mr. Scary closed his eyes.

I put my head back down on my desk.

He covered me up with my sweatshirt.

I appreciated that.

14

2

Candy Corn

That afternoon, I zoomed to my house from the bus stop. And I ran in my front door as fast as lightning.

"*TATTLETALE!* T-A-T-T-L-E-T-A-L-E SPELLS *TATTLETALE!*" I hollered.

After that, I used the word in a sentence.

"*TATTLETALE* . . . MAY IS A BIG FAT *TATTLETALE!*"

I heard my grandma's voice.

"Junie B., honey? Is that you?" she called. "I'm in Ollie's room! Come back and see us!"

I circled my hands around my mouth.

"OKAY!" I hollered again. "O-K SPELLS *OKAY*!"

After that, I hurried back there very fast. And I hugged my grandma real tight.

"Did you hear me spell *tattletale*?" I said. "I looked that word up in my dictionary at school. On account of May tattletaled on me today."

Grandma Miller was changing Ollie's clothes. She shook her head at that news.

"Oh, dear . . . not more trouble with May," she said. "Honestly, Junie B. You're just going to have to ignore that girl."

I crossed my arms.

"Yeah, only how can I even ignore her when she calls me a scaredy-cat baby?" I said. "She told *all* the children that I am scared of Halloween, Grandma! Only if

May knew what I know about Halloween, she would be scared, too."

Grandma looked curious at me.

"What are you talking about?" she asked. "What is it that you know?"

I swallowed very hard. Then I made my voice quieter.

"I know five scary secrets . . . *that's* what I know," I said. "Only I'm not even allowed to tell anyone. Or else my head will turn into a wart."

Chills came on my arms.

"Paulie Allen Puffer told me that," I whispered even softer.

Grandma Miller wrinkled her eyebrows.

"Paulie Allen Puffer?" she said. "Wasn't he the boy who told you that a monster lived under your bed?"

I nodded my head.

"Yes. That's the exact same Paulie Allen Puffer," I said. "He knows lots of scary stuff, Grandma. On account of Paulie Allen Puffer has a brother who's in eighth grade. And eighth grade is almost as old as a grown-up."

Grandma did a little smile. Then she finished buttoning Ollie's sweater. And she put him on the floor to walk to me.

Ollie does not walk that professional.

He teeters and totters and weevils and wobbles.

He fell down on my foot.

Then he patted my shoe very nice. And he said the word *moo*.

Moo is Ollie's favorite word.

He is not the sharpest tool in the barn.

Grandma bent down to pick him up.

I touched her softie white hair.

Bats would love that hair, I believe.

"I wouldn't go out on Halloween if I were you, Grandma," I said. "Not with *that* head of hair."

Grandma Miller did a little frown. Then she fluffed her hair very much.

"Why? What's wrong with my hair?" she asked. "Don't you like it?"

I zipped my lips shut. 'Cause I said too much already, I think.

Grandma Miller fluffed some more.

"Speaking of Halloween, your mother is coming home from work early today. She wants to take you to the store to buy your costume."

Just then, more chills came on my arms.

I started backing out of Ollie's room very slow.

"Yeah, only I might not want to buy my costume today," I said. "I might want to buy it tomorrow . . . or the next day . . . or never, possibly."

I kept on backing up.

"Okay. Well, I think I will go take a nap now, Grandma. And so when Mother gets home, please tell her not to bother me."

I did a salute.

"Thank you and good night," I said.

After that, I turned around. And I ran to my room. And I quick closed the door.

A second later, I opened it a tiny crack.

"Yeah, only don't forget what I told you," I called. "Do *not* go out with that head of hair on Halloween. 'Cause that is just *asking* for trouble, Helen!"

Grandma Miller called back at me.

She said please do not call her Helen.

I shut my door again.

Then I picked up my favorite stuffed animal named Philip Johnny Bob. And I hurried to get in bed.

"If we pretend to be asleep, maybe I won't have to go to the scary Halloween store with Mother," I told him.

Philip quick pretended to snore.

I tapped on him.

"Yeah, only she's not actually home yet, Phil," I explained. "Plus I need to tell you the five scary secrets. 'Cause I can't tell them to real, actual people. But you don't count, probably. 'Cause your ears aren't really real."

Philip Johnny Bob felt his ears with his front foot.

Really? You're kidding me! he said. *My ears aren't real? Are you sure? Because they really, really feel real, don't you think?*

I felt his ears.

"Yes, Philip. They *do* feel real. But they're just made out of cloth."

Philip Johnny Bob kept feeling his ears. And so finally I had to take his foot away.

After that, I made my voice into a whisper. And I told him the five scary secrets.

First, I whispered the secret about the monsters and the witches.

Then I whispered the secrets about the pumpkins and the bats and the cats.

And finally, I whispered the secret about how candy corn is not actually corn.

His mouth came open at that one.

No! he said. *That can't be true. Candy corn has got to be corn. It has corn right in its exact name. Plus it even looks like corn, kind of. And so if it isn't corn, what kind of vegetable is it?*

I did a shrug. "I don't know, Phil," I said. "It can't be peas. 'Cause peas are roundish and greenish."

Right, said Philip. *And it can't be carrots. 'Cause carrots are longish and crunchish.*

We thought some more.

Then both of us looked at each other.

"Maybe Paulie Allen Puffer's big brother is wrong about the corn," I said.

Yes. He's got to be wrong, said Philip. *Candy corn is definitely corn. There's nothing else it could be.*

I nodded. "But the other scary secrets are true, I bet. You can just *tell* they're true by the sound of them. Like why would a real, actual monster put on a costume if he already looks like he's wearing one?"

I know, said Philip. *And the pointy, sharp pumpkin teeth make sense, too. 'Cause what good are pointy, sharp teeth if you can't eat feet?*

"Right," I said. "And you *know* the bat and cat secrets are true, too. 'Cause what bat wouldn't want to live in Grandma's softie hair?"

And witches' cats can definitely claw you into shreddle, said Philip.

He looked up at me.

Maybe you shouldn't go trick-or-treating this year, Junie B., he said. *Maybe you should just stay here with me . . . all safe and sound . . . right in your own house.*

I hugged him very tight.

That elephant is very supportive.

3

■ ■ ■ ■ ■ ■ ■ ■ ■ ■

Squirty

Me and Philip Johnny Bob took a real nap.

It was an accident.

'Cause both of us are too old for naps.

But sometimes naps just happen.

After we woke up, Mother came in my room. And she kissed my cheek hello.

I did a yawn and waved.

Mother ruffled my hair.

"I know you're still sleepy, honey. But we need to go get your Halloween costume now," she said. "Grandma's going to stay with Ollie while we're gone."

My tummy did a flip-flop at that news.

I had to get out of this. I just *had* to.

"Yeah, only I don't actually *feel* like getting my Halloween costume right now," I said, real whiny. "And anyway, I don't even know what I want to be yet."

After that, I quick pulled my covers over my head.

"I will think about this and get back to you tomorrow," I said.

Mother did a laugh.

Then she pulled my covers off again.

"Sorry, Junie B. But we can't wait until tomorrow," she said. "Tomorrow is Halloween."

After that, she picked me up from my bed. And she stood me on the floor.

"I'm sure that once we get to the store, you'll find lots of fun costumes to choose from," she said. "Now please put on your shoes while I go get my coat."

After she left, I grabbed Philip Johnny Bob very panicked.

"She's going to make me do it, Philip! Mother's going to make me go trick-or-treating tomorrow night! And that means I'm going to see real, actual monsters and witches! Plus I'll probably be coming home with a bat in my hair."

I ran around my room very upset.

Philip watched me go.

Why don't you just tell her, Junie B.? he asked. *If you tell Mother the five scary secrets, then she won't make you go trick-or-treating, I bet.*

I shook my head.

"But I *can't*, Philip," I said. "I can't tell *anyone* the five secrets, or else my head will get turned into a wart. Remember that?"

I made a sick face. "A wart would be a hard head to explain."

Philip thought some more.

Okay, then make up a different reason why you can't go, he said. *Tell Mother you're afraid of the dark.*

I rolled my eyes way up at the ceiling.

"But I'm *not* afraid of the dark, Philip. I'm not afraid of anything, usually."

I paused for a second.

"Except for roosters with pointy lips, of course," I said. "But that is to be expected."

I tapped on my chin.

"Also, I do not care for ponies who stomple you to death," I said.

And clowns, Philip said. *You're also afraid of clowns.*

I looked at him kind of annoyed.

"Yes, Phil. But *everyone* is afraid of clowns," I said. "Even *Grandma Miller* is afraid of clowns."

I thought back.

"Remember when all of us went to the circus together? And that scary, mean clown chased Grandma around the bleachers with his seltzer bottle?"

Philip nodded. *Yes. Squirty the Clown,* he said. *He made Grandma wear an unattractive balloon hat. Remember that?*

"Of course I remember," I said. "I still have bad dreams about that clown. Even monsters and witches would run away from Squirty, I bet."

Sure they would, said Philip. *Squirty would scare the pants off those guys.*

I did a sigh.

"Lucky Squirty," I said. "Squirty the Clown doesn't have to be afraid of *anything,* probably."

Just then, Mother's voice hollered down the hall.

"JUNIE B., ARE YOU READY YET? YOU NEED TO GET A MOVE ON, HONEY. WE'VE GOT TO GO!"

Me and Philip looked frantic at each other.

Then, bingo!

A miracle happened!

And it's called, the answer to my problem popped right into my head!

I springed up as fast as a spring.

"Hey! Wait a second! I know the answer, Philip! I know what I can be for Halloween!"

I danced around real joyful.

"I can be *Squirty*!" I said. "I can be *Squirty the Clown*! Then I can squirt the monsters and witches with my seltzer bottle! And then they will run away!"

I grabbed Philip Johnny Bob. And we twirled all around.

"SQUIRTY! SQUIRTY! SQUIRTY!" we sang real happy.

Mother heard us being noisy. And she hurried into my room.

"Hey, hey, hey! What's going on in here?" she asked.

I ran and hugged her legs.

"I'm going to be Squirty! *That's* what's going on here!" I hollered.

Mother stood there for a real long time.

Then, all of a sudden, her face went funny.

"Oh, dear . . . *no*. You don't mean

Squirty the *Clown* . . . do you?" she asked.
She closed her eyes.

"Not that nasty little clown who chased your grandmother around the bleachers with a seltzer bottle?"

I laughed and clapped and laughed and clapped.

"Yes, Mother! Yes, yes, yes! That's *'zactly* the Squirty I mean!"

Mother shook her head.

"But . . . but this makes no *sense*, Junie B. You were scared to pieces by Squirty. Why would you want to be such a terrible clown for Halloween?"

"*Because!*" I said. "Because I'm not allowed to *tell* you, that's why! But I really, really want to be Squirty!"

After that, I quick put on my shoes.

And I grabbed my jacket.

And I ran out to the car.

I honked the horn for Mother.

'Cause when you're a mean clown with a seltzer bottle, trick-or-treating doesn't worry you a bit!

And so HA HA on monsters.

And HA HA on witches and bats and cats!

And HA HA on scary Halloween!

4

■ ■ ■ ■ ■ ■ ■ ■ ■

The Halloween Store

The Halloween store was in the mall.

I pulled Mother there in a jiffy.

Only too bad for me.

'Cause as soon as I saw the store, I screeched on my brakes speedy quick. On account of the stuff in the window gave me the creeps, I tell you!

The window was filled with skeletons and devils. Plus there were scary, hairy monster heads all over the place!

I closed my eyes real tight. And I did a hard swallow.

'Cause scary, hairy monster heads can take the brave right out of you.

I squeezed Mother's hand tighter.

"Okay, here's a little change of plans," I said. "I think I will go home now."

Then I tried to pull Mother back the other way. But she didn't budge.

"I know those masks *look* scary," she said. "But rubber masks can't hurt you, Junie B."

She smiled. "Those masks are made from the same kind of rubber that Ollie's rubber ducky is made from. And you're not afraid of Rubber Ducky, are you?"

I rolled my eyes at that dumb question.

"Rubber Ducky doesn't have a sword through his head," I said.

Mother didn't listen.

She pulled me into the store. And we went to the aisle with the little girls' costumes.

I looked up and down the shelves.

They had every little costume in the book, I tell you!

They had Little Red Riding Hood, and Little Bo-Peep, and Mary Had a Little Lamb, and Little Orphan Annie, and the Little Mermaid. Plus also, they had Little Miss Muppet Who Sat on Her Trumpet!

Mother's face got gleamy and happy.

"Oh, don't you just *love* these, Junie B.?" she asked. "Wouldn't you like to wear one of these darling costumes tomorrow?"

I smiled very pleasant.

"No thank you," I said.

Just then, a store lady walked by.

I reached out and tapped on her.

"Where's the Squirty suits?" I asked.

The lady looked curious at me. Then she looked at Mother.

"Did she say *squirrelly* suits?" she asked.

Mother closed her eyes a second.

"No. I'm afraid she said *Squirty* suits,"

she told her. "Squirty the Clown. He sprays old women with seltzer."

The lady looked strange at us.

Then she led me and Mother to the clown stuff. And she went the other way.

I looked down the clown row real nervous.

And oh no! Oh no!

There were scary clown parts hanging everywhere, I tell you!

I quick jumped behind Mother's skirt.

Then very slow, I peeked out.

There were round clown noses. And creepy clown hair. And big white clown

gloves. And giant, baggy clown pants with s'penders on them.

I did some deep breaths.

Then finally, I came out from behind Mother. And I looked all the way down the aisle.

"Yeah, only here's the problem. I don't actually see the Squirty suits," I said.

Mother patted me. "Yes, well, I didn't think we'd find a *real* Squirty costume," she said. "But with all of these clown parts, you can be much cuter than Squirty, Junie B."

She took a wig off the shelf and plopped it on my head.

"Here, how 'bout this funny, frizzy red hair?" she said.

I quick took it off.

"No, Mother. No!" I said. "I don't *want* to be *frizzy*! I want to be *Squirty*!"

I stamped my foot.

"Squirty! Squirty!" I said. "I *have* to be Squirty!"

"Shh! Honestly, Junie B.! What has gotten into you?" she said very snappish.

Just then, a boy walked by. And he saw me getting snapped at.

I asked Mother to tone it down a notch.

I will not be saying that comment again, probably.

Her face turned steamy mad. And she talked through closed teeth.

"That's enough out of you, young lady," she said. "Not one more rude word! Do you understand me?"

I rocked back and forth on my feet kind of nervous.

Then I did a gulp.

"Yeah, only that is really going to cut

down on my end of the conversation," I said kind of quiet.

Mother looked at me a minute. Then she quick covered her mouth with her hand.

She was doing a grin back there, I think.

After that, her voice got nicer.

"You've *got* to listen to me about this costume business, Junie B.," she said. "There . . . are . . . *no* . . . *Squirty* . . . *suits,* okay? They don't even *make* Squirty suits. Squirty is *not* a famous clown."

I felt shocked at that information.

"But . . . but how can he not be famous, Mother?" I said. "I know that clown like the front of my hand."

Mother nodded. "Yes, well, I'm afraid Squirty made a strong impression on *all* of us. And why you're determined to be such a terrible clown is a total puzzle to me," she said. "But if you really, really want to be Squirty, the best we can do is to get you an outfit that is *similar* to his."

My shoulders slumped very much.

'Cause *similar* does not mean *exactly*.

Mother looked at her watch.

"It's your choice, Junie B. We either buy you an outfit similar to Squirty's . . . or we buy you a Little Bo-Peep costume."

I did a sad sigh.

Then I walked down the aisle very glum.

And I looked for a *similar* seltzer bottle.

5

No Squirty

Dear little piece of paper that
I am writing on in my room,
  Today is Halloween.
  Only guess what?
  NO seltzer bottle! THAT'S
WHAT!
  'Cause Mother said I am not
even allowed to squirt people!
  And so how am I supposed to
scare off the monsters and

witches? That's what I would
like to know!

   Also, my clown hair is not
exactly like Squirty's. Plus I
couldn't even find a Squirty
shirt.

   I do not have faith in this
costume.

                   From,

                 Not exactly Squirty

P.S. I would like to spray
Mother with ~~seltser~~ seltzer.

I stopped writing and looked at my clock.
   It was already after dinner.
   Mother was in Ollie's room.

She was dressing him in his Halloween costume.

I crawled under my covers with Philip Johnny Bob. And I worried about my costume some more.

"I still don't know why I can't squirt monsters with seltzer," I said.

Me either, Philip said. *Squirting seltzer would scare their pants off.*

Just then, we heard a knock on my door.

I did not say *come in.* But Mother came in anyway.

That is a bad habit of hers.

I peeked my eyes out of the covers.

Mother was holding baby Ollie. He was wearing a cow suit. My grandma Miller made it for him for Halloween.

Mother put Ollie on the floor.

"Moo," he said.

I made the cuckoo sign at him.

"Come on, Junie B. Let's go," said Mother. "Without Daddy here to help, I'm running behind. We have to hurry and get you dressed. Grandma and Grampa Miller are coming over to take pictures."

After that, she got my bag of clown parts. And she spread them on the bed.

There was a red clown nose. And curly clown hair. And big, fat clown pants with s'penders.

Also, there was a giant bow tie like Squirty wore. And big white gloves. And a shirt with puffery buttons on the front.

Mother fastened the buttons of my clown shirt. And she pulled the clown pants over my jeans.

Then she put the s'penders over my shoulders. And she snapped the bow tie around my neck. And I put on my gloves.

I looked at myself in the mirror.

"But . . . but I don't look like Squirty," I said real whiny. "I just look like plain old me . . . except with very stupid taste in clothes."

Mother smiled. "Well, of course you don't look like a clown *yet,* silly," she said. "You can't look like a clown until you've got your makeup on."

After that, she turned me around to face her. And she told me to close my eyes. And she put clown makeup all over my face.

When she got done, she plopped my clown hair on my head.

And then, kerplunk!

She stuck on my red nose. And she beamed real happy.

"Ta-daa!" she said. "You're a clown!"

My heart got poundy and thumpy at those words.

I turned around to see in the mirror again.

And wowie wow wow!

My eyes popped right out of my head!

'Cause I looked like *Squirty*, I tell you!

I did a loud gasp at that sight.

Then I bent over and tried to catch my breath.

"Whew!" I said. "Whoa! Whew!"

Mother laughed.

"I'll take that as a compliment," she said. "I have to admit, you look a lot more like Squirty than I thought you would."

I kept on breathing till I got my air back.

Then, very slow, I raised my head. And I peeked at myself once more.

Chill bumps came on my arms.

I leaned closer and made a creepy clown grin.

I did a shiver.

"I am scaring myself silly," I said.

Just then, the doorbell rang.

It was my grandma and grampa, I think!

Mother picked up Ollie the Cow. And she hurried to let them in.

I stayed behind to look at myself some more.

I waved in the mirror with my big clown glove.

Then I backed up a little bit. And I pretended to squirt myself with seltzer.

"Squirt!" I said. "Squirt! Squirt! Squirt!"

Very fast, I spun around. And I squirted my Raggedy Ann named Ruth. And my Raggedy Andy named Larry. And my teddy named Teddy.

"Squirt! Squirt! Squirt!" I said again.

Finally, I put down my pretend squirt bottle. And I sat on the edge of my bed.

"Darn it," I said. "I wish I had a *real* squirt bottle. 'Cause if monsters aren't afraid of my clown face, then how else will I scare them away?"

I walked back and forth very pacing.

Just then, I heard Grandma Miller's voice in the hall.

She was giggling about Ollie in his cow suit. And so I couldn't wait for her to see me, too!

All of a sudden, I got a funny idea in my head.

I did a sneaky smile in my mirror.

Then, very quiet, I tippytoed out of my room. And I creeped down the hall on softie clown feet.

And then, HA!

I springed out at Grandma with all my might!

And I did my scariest scream!

"AAAAA! AAAAA! AAAAA!" I screamed. "AAAAA! AAAAA! AAAAA!"

Grandma jumped way high in the air!

Mother jumped, too!

I laughed and laughed at that funny sight.

Then I ran all around them. And I kept on screaming.

"AAAAA! AAAAA! I'M A SCREAMY CLOWN! I'M A SCREAMY CLOWN!"

Just then, Grampa Miller came through the front door.

I ran at him very speedy. And I butted him in the stomach with my clown head.

Then WHOA!

Mother grabbed me by my clown pants.

"For heaven's sake, Junie B.! Knock it off!" she yelled.

I stopped screaming. And I tapped on her very polite.

"Yeah, only I'm not actually Junie B.," I explained. "I'm a screamy clown."

I stood there a second.

Then my whole face lighted up!

"Hey! Hold it! That's a good name for me, Mother!"

I clapped real excited.

"If I can't be Squirty, I can be Screamy!" I said. "I can be Screamy the Clown!"

After that, I ran to get my Halloween bag. And I laughed some more.

'Cause Screamy the Clown can scare the pants off people, I bet!

Even *without* seltzer!

6

■ ■ ■ ■ ■ ■ ■ ■ ■ ■ ■

Trick-or-Fruit

Mother put Ollie in his stroller. And she took us trick-or-treating.

She tried to hold my hand. But I quick pulled it away.

"Yeah, only I'm not even a scaredy-cat baby," I said. "I am Screamy the Clown."

After that, I speeded up my feet. And I walked very fast in front of those two.

Our first neighbor's house is where grouchy Mrs. Morty lives.

Grouchy Mrs. Morty lives all by herself with grouchy Mr. Morty.

Their yard has lots of lawn decorations in it. Only do not accidentally take a little elf from their garden. Or else grouchy Mrs. Morty will threaten to call the cops.

I ran up their porch steps.

There was a big trick-or-treat boy already there.

He was ringing the doorbell.

I looked at him very close.

He was wearing fishing boots and a fishing pole.

I waved at him with my clown gloves.

"Hello. How are you today? I am Screamy the Clown," I said. "And I can scare the pants off people."

The boy rolled his eyes at me. He didn't say any words.

I pulled on his fishing pole very friendly.

"So what are you dressed as?" I asked.

The boy sucked his cheeks into his head.

"I'm a fisherman, you clown," he said.

Fishermen have an attitude, apparently.

That's how come I decided to scare the pants off that guy.

I did a creepy clown grin.

Then I stood on my tallest tippytoes.

And I screamed right in his face.

"AAAAA! AAAAA! AAAAA!" I screamed.

Just then, grouchy Mrs. Morty opened the front door. And she quick held her ears.

"JUNIE B. JONES! MY WORD! STOP ALL THAT RACKET!"

I stopped my racket.

"Yeah, only I'm not actually Junie B. Jones," I explained. "I am Screamy the Clown. And Screamy the Clown can scare the pants off people."

The fisherman boy rolled his eyes again. "I don't even know this clown," he said.

I tapped on grouchy Mrs. Morty's arm.

"Trick-or-treat. Trick-or-treat. Give me something good to eat," I sang very amusing.

Grouchy Mrs. Morty picked up a big bowl. And she gave us each an apple.

It plopped very hard in the bottom of my bag.

I stared down at that thing.

"Okey-doke . . . here is the problem, Mrs. Morty. I already have apples at my house," I said.

I did a little frown.

"Also, I didn't say trick-or-*fruit*," I said.

The fisherman boy laughed real loud.

Then he leaned over next to me.

And he dropped his apple down my

clown pants. And he quick ran off the
porch.

I stood there very shocked.

"Okay. That is not actually acceptable,"
I said kind of mumbly.

Just then, Mother came up the steps
with Ollie the Cow.

Mrs. Morty's face got nicer.

She patted Ollie's cow head. And she gave him a Rice Krispies Treat.

I looked curious at that woman.

"Okay, see . . . I didn't actually know that Rice Krispies Treats were available," I said. "And so I would like to trade in these apples, please."

I reached into my bag and my clown pants. And I tried to give the apples back.

But grouchy Mrs. Morty did a grump face.

"I only made *Treats* for little ones," she said.

After that, she patted Ollie again. And she closed the door.

Mother stared at me.

"My . . . that went well. It's only the first house, and you've already had an apple dropped down your pants," she said.

"Not *Creamy . . . Screamy!*" I hollered. "I'm Screamy the Clown. And I can scare the pants off you!"

Then I made more claws. And I jumped up and down very frightening.

"BOO!" I shouted. "BOO . . . and I MEAN it!"

They looked at each other and did more shrugs.

Cinderella started walking again.

"Sorry, Creamy. But you're just not scary," she said.

The Fairy Godmother nodded. "You're making a fool out of yourself, sister," she said.

Then she bonked me on the head with her wand. And she started walking, too.

I stood there real glum.

Pretty soon, Mother and Ollie caught up with me.

Mother said I am acting like a lunatic. And I have to stay with her and Ollie.

Then she held my s'penders so I couldn't run away anymore.

My shoulders slumped very much.

"Yeah, only why would I even run away again?" I said. "'Cause I can't scare a flea, I tell you."

I glanced down at my big, fat pants.

"I look like a clown in this getup," I said real embarrassed.

I did not feel brave anymore.

Finally, Mother let go of my s'penders and she held my hand.

I walked real slow and nervous. And I looked for monsters in the dark.

Also, I swatted at the air over my head. Or else a bat might land in my clown wig.

Mother kept on pulling me.

"Come on, Junie B. Move your feet," she said.

Just then, I heard voices behind me.

I quick spun around.

And OH NO! OH NO!

IT WAS A WITCH! A witch was behind me on the sidewalk! And she was walking with a skeleton guy!

I quick yanked my hand away from

Mother! And I dived behind a bush!

"SCATTER, PEOPLE! SCATTER!" I yelled.

"Junie B.! Come back!" called Mother.

My heart pounded and pounded. But I did not go back.

Instead, I crouched into a teensy clown ball. And I peeked through the bush branches.

The witch was wearing a pointy black witch hat. And a long black witch dress.

She passed Mother on the sidewalk.

"Hello," said Mother.

"MOO!" said Ollie.

The witch laughed at him.

"I think he means *boo*," she said to the skeleton.

Then both of them laughed some more.

And they kept on walking.

I flopped on my back very relieved.

"Whew," I said. "That was a close one."

Then I wiped my nervous head. And I tried to calm my breathing.

Only too bad for me.

'Cause—all of a sudden—Mother came running around the bush.

And she got me by my s'penders again.

And this time . . . she didn't let go.

8

Candy

Dear little candy wrapper that
I am writing on with my new
pencil,
   Halloween was a very long
night.
   After the witch, we saw two
monsters and three more
witches.
   Witches are big candy eaters,
apparently
~~aparently.~~

I hid behind Mother till they were gone.

Ollie mooed at them.

Cows are braver than they look.

From,

Junie B. Jones

After I finished writing, I pulled off my clown nose. And I did a breath of fresh air.

"I am glad that night is over," I said real relieved.

Just then, Grampa Miller came in my room to say goodbye.

He and Grandma were going to the airport to pick up my daddy from his business trip.

Only bad news. 'Cause Daddy wouldn't be home till after I was asleep. So I couldn't even see him till morning.

I hugged Grampa very tight. And I gave him my trail mix to eat in the car.

Frank Miller will eat anything.

Mother was giving Ollie a bath.

I dumped my Halloween bag out on my bed. And I lined up my stuffed animals to look at it.

Whoa, said my Raggedy Andy named Larry. *You got a million candy bars, almost.*

Yes, said my Raggedy Ann named Ruth. *Too bad about the dumb apples and raisins. But the rest of it looks good.*

"I know," I said. "Mother took Ollie and me on four entire streets. It was very scary. But I made a good haul."

Philip looked at me kind of surprised. *It*

was scary? he asked. *How come it was scary? I thought you were being Screamy.*

I sighed very tired.

"Yeah, only nobody was afraid of Screamy," I said. "Not even a fisherman or dumb Cinderella or her crazy old Fairy Godmother."

After that, all of my stuffed animals hopped in my lap. And we did a group hug.

Don't worry, said Philip Johnny Bob. *You will be braver next year, I bet.*

I nodded. "Yes," I said. "Next year I will be a cow."

After that, I started to count my candy.

Philip did a gasp.

Peanuts? he said. *Is that peanuts I see?*

I did a giggle.

Then I opened up the peanuts. And I put one in Philip's trunk.

It fell out again.

Shoot, said Philip.

I tried two more times. Then I took him to my desk. And I taped the peanut in there.

Mmm, he said. *Delicious.*

After that, I gave a peanut to Larry and Ruth and Teddy. And I ate the rest myself. Also, I ate a gummy worm. And I chewed my pack of sugarless gum.

After a while, Mother called to me from Ollie's room.

"Junie B., did you wash your face and take off your costume yet? It's really late, honey. You've got to get to bed."

I shut my door very quiet. 'Cause I was too sleepy to wash my face, that's why.

I quick took off my clown pants. And I crawled under my covers.

"I'm already *in* bed, Mother!" I called back.

I yawned very sleepy.

"I'm going to sleep now, okay? See you in the morning!"

Then I turned out my light. And I pulled the sheet way over my head so Mother wouldn't see that I didn't wash my face.

My eyes felt heavy and pooped.

I did another yawn.

Then I went right to sleep.

And I dreamed I was a cow.

9

■ ■ ■ ■ ■ ■ ■ ■ ■ ■

Welcome Home!

In the middle of my dream, I thought I heard my door open.

I opened my sleepy eyes a teeny bit.

"Junie B.?" whispered a voice.

It was still dark in my room.

I rolled over to see who was talking.

Then, all of a sudden, the voice yelled real loud.

"AAAH!" it said.

I sat straight up!

My heart pounded and pounded.

Someone was standing next to my bed!

I squinted to see who it was.
And guess what?
I think it was my *daddy*!
He was standing in the dark!

And his hand was over his mouth!

And he was looking at my scary clown face.

"Daddy?" I whispered. "Is that you?"

"*Junie B.?* Is that *you*?" Daddy whispered back.

He turned on my light.

"Oh my gosh!" he said. "No *wonder* you startled me. You still have your makeup on!"

Just then, Mother came hurrying into my room.

"Junie B. Jones, I *told* you to wash that clown makeup off," she said. "You could have scared your poor daddy to death."

Daddy was patting his heart with his hand.

"Sorry, Daddy. Sorry I scared you," I said. "Sorry, sorry, sorry."

After that, I sat there for a second.

Then my mouth did a little grin.

"Did I *really* scare you, Daddy? Huh? Did I? You're not just saying that, are you? I really, really scared you . . . right?"

Mother looked annoyed at me.

"My goodness, Junie B. I've never seen anyone who is so *thrilled* about scaring people. It's not a very nice thing to do, you know."

She quick grabbed a tissue and tried to wipe my clown face off.

"Great," she said. "All this does is make you smudgy."

I giggled at that funny word.

Then I peeked around her at Daddy.

"Boo! I'm Smudgy!" I said. "I'm Smudgy the Clown!"

Daddy raised up his eyebrows.

"Oh, you are, are you?" he said.

Then he quick plopped on my bed. And we tickled each other very silly.

After we got done, we hugged and hugged very much. 'Cause I missed that guy, I tell you!

I showed Daddy all my Halloween stuff.

"If it wasn't for those dumb apples and raisins, I'd have a hundred percent candy now," I explained.

And so wait till you hear this!

Daddy said he would eat my raisins!

And Mother said she would eat my apples!

And so now my candy is one hundred percent *perfect*!

Finally, Mother put all my candy bars back in my bag. And she washed my face with a washcloth.

Then she and Daddy tucked me back into bed. And they closed my door.

Only here is the bestest thing of all.

'Cause as soon as Mother was gone, Daddy quick opened my door again. And he whispered a quiet secret.

"Psst," he said real soft. "You scared the *pants* off me, Junie B. Jones."

I giggled at that nice compliment.

Then I hugged Philip Johnny Bob real happy.

And I smiled myself to sleep.

BARBARA PARK is one of today's funniest, most popular authors. Her middle-grade novels, which include *Skinnybones, The Kid in the Red Jacket, My Mother Got Married (And Other Disasters),* and *Mick Harte Was Here,* have won over forty children's book awards. Barbara holds a B.S. in education from the University of Alabama. She has two grown sons and lives with her husband, Richard, in Arizona.

DENISE BRUNKUS'S entertaining illustrations have appeared in over fifty books. She lives in New Jersey with her husband and daughter.